C000064825

THE RAVEN

the RAVEN LOU REED

THE RAVEN

LYRICS AND TEXT BY LOU REED

WITH PHOTOGRAPHS BY JULIAN SCHNABEL

GROVE PRESS
NEW YORK

Published simultaneously in Canada
Printed in the United States of America

FIRST EDITION

Library of Congress Cataloging-in-Publication Data
Reed, Lou.
    [Raven. Libretto]
    The raven / lyrics and text by Lou Reed ; with photographs by Julian
Schnabel.
      p. cm.
    Libretto of a studio adaptation of the musical POEtry.
    ISBN 0-8021-1756-2 (hc edition)
    ISBN 0-8021-1759-7 (limited slipcase edition)
    1. Musicals—Librettos.   I. Reed, Lou. POEtry.   II. Poe, Edgar Allan,
1809–1849.   III. Title.
    ML50.R317R43 2003
    782.1'40268—dc21   2003051151

Grove Press
841 Broadway
New York, NY 10003

03   04   05   06   07   10 9 8 7 6 5 4 3 2 1

Acknowledgments

To Robert Wilson, our original stage director, whose idea this was.

To Hal Willner, my coproducer of the reworked audio version of this play.

THE RAVEN

This is a work for the imagination; therefore I have included only audio cues, as this version is meant to be heard in the mind.

Speakers (in order of appearance)

VOICE
OLD POE
YOUNG POE
LIGEIA
ROWENA
LENORE
POE
DEATH
RODERICK USHER
LADY MADELINE OF USHER
ENTERTAINER
POE ENSEMBLE
THE OLD MAN
FIVE POLICEMEN
FEMALE TEACHER
MALE STUDENT
MOTHER
DAUGHTER
JUDGES
DEAD PEOPLE
HOP-FROG
KING
TRIPITENA, A PRINCESS

THE CONQUEROR WORM

VOICE
Lo! It's a gala night.
A mystic throng bedecked
Sit in a theater to see
A play of hopes and fears
While the orchestra breathes fitfully
The music of the spheres.

Minds mutter and mumble low—
Mere puppets they, who come and go
Disguised as gods,
They shift the scenery to and fro
Inevitably trapped by invisible woe.

This motley drama—to be sure—
Will not be forgotten.
A phantom chased for evermore,
Never seized by the crowd
Though they circle—
Returning to the same spot—
Circle and return
To the selfsame spot
Always to the selfsame spot,
With much of madness and more of sin,

And horror and mimic rout
The soul of the plot.

Out—out are the lights—out all!
And over each dying form
The curtain, a funeral pall,
Comes with the rush of a storm.
The angels, haggard and wan,
Unveiling and uprising affirm
That the play is the tragedy, "Man,"
And its hero the conqueror worm.

Instrumental overture

ACT I

OLD POE

Guitar melody

OLD POE

As I look back on my life—if I could have the glorious moment—the wondrous opportunity to comprehend—the chance to see my younger self one time—to converse . . . to hear his thoughts. . . .

Cello melody—continues throughout speech

YOUNG POE

In the science of the mind there is no point more thrilling than to notice (which I never noticed in schools) that in our endeavors to recall to memory something long-forgotten we often find ourselves upon the very verge of remembrance without being in the end able to remember. Under the intense scrutiny of Ligeia's eyes, I have felt the full knowledge and force of their expression and yet been unable to possess it and have felt it leave me as so many other things have left—the letter half-read, the bottle half-drunk—finding in the commonest objects of the universe a circle of analogies, of metaphors for that expression which had been willfully withheld from me, the access to the inner soul denied.

Eyes blazed with a too-glorious effulgence, pale fingers transparent, waxen, the hue of the grave. Blue veins upon the lofty forehead swelled and sunk impetuously with the tides of deep emotion and I saw that she must die, that she was wrestling with the dark shadow. Her stern nature had impressed me with the belief that, to her, death would come without its terrors—but not so. I groaned in anguish at the pitiable spectacle. I would have soothed. I would have reasoned. But she was amid the most convulsive of writhings. Oh, pitiful soul. Her voice more gentle, more low, and yet her words grew wilder of meaning. I reeled, entranced, to a melody more than mortal.

She loved me, no doubt, and in her bosom love reigned as no ordinary passion. But in death only was I impressed with the intensity of her affection. Her more than passionate devotion amounted to idolatry. How had I deserved to be so blessed and then so cursed with the removal of my beloved upon the hour of her most delirious musings?

In her more than womanly abandonment to love, all unmerited and unworthily bestowed, I came to realize the principle of her longing. It was a yearning for life, an eager, intense desire for life, which was now fleeing so rapidly away as she returned solemnly to her bed of death. And I had no utterance capable of expressing it, except to say, Man doth not yield to the angels, nor unto death utterly, save only through the weakness of his feeble will.

I became wild with the excitement of an immoderate dose of opium. I saw her raising wine to her lips or may have dreamed that I saw fall within a goblet, as if from some invisible spring in the atmosphere of the room, three or four large drops of a brilliant and ruby-colored fluid. Falling. While Ligeia lay in her bed of ebony—the bed of death—with mine eyes riveted upon her body. Then came a moan, a sob low and gentle but once. I listened in superstitious terror but heard it not again. I strained vision to see any motion in the corpse, but there was not the slightest perceptible. Yet I had heard the noise and my whole soul was awakened within me. The red liquid fell and I thought, Ligeia lives, and I felt my brain reel, my heart cease to beat, and my limbs go rigid where I sat. In extremity of horror I heard a vague sound issuing from the region of the bed. Rushing to her I saw—I distinctly saw—a tremor upon her lips. I sprang to my feet and chafed and bathed the temples and hands but in vain; all color fled, all pulsation ceased. Her lips resumed the expression of the dead, the icy hue, the sunken outline, and all the loathsome peculiarities of that which for many days has been the tenant of the tomb.

And again I sank into visions of Ligeia. And again I heard a low sob. And as I looked she seemed to grow taller. What inexpressible madness seized me with that thought? I ran to touch her. Her head fell, and her clothing crumbled, and there streamed forth huge masses of long disheveled hair.

It was blacker than the raven wings of midnight.

EDGAR ALLAN POE

YOUNG POE
These are the stories of Edgar Allan Poe
Not exactly the boy next door

He'll tell you tales of horror
Then he'll play with your mind
If you haven't heard of him
You must be deaf or blind.

These are the stories of Edgar Allan Poe
Not exactly the boy next door

He'll tell you about Usher
Whose house burned in his mind
His love for his dear sister
(Whose death would drive him wild)
The murder of a stranger
The murder of a friend
The callings from the pits of hell
That never seem to end.

These are the stories of Edgar Allan Poe
Not exactly the boy next door

These are the stories of Edgar Allan Poe
Not exactly the boy next door

The diabolic image of the city and the sea
The chaos and the carnage that reside deep within me
Decapitations—poisonings—hellish not a bore
You won't need 3-D glasses to pass beyond this door.

These are the stories of Edgar Allan Poe
Not exactly the boy next door

No Nosferatu Vincent Price or naked women here
A mind unfurled a mind unbent is all that we have here
Truth, fried orangutans flutter to the stage
Leave your expectations home
And listen to the stories of Edgar Allan Poe.

We give you the soliloquy the raven at the door
The flaming pits the moving walls no equilibrium
No ballast, no bombast, the unvarnished truth we've got
A mind that swoons guiltily
Cooking ravings in a pot.

These are the stories of Edgar Allan Poe
Not exactly the boy next door.

A telltale heart a rotting cask
A valley of unrest
A conqueror worm devouring souls
Keep the best for last
The bells that ring for Annie Lee
As Poe's buried alive
Regretting his beloved's death in all her
Many guises.

These are the stories of Edgar Allan Poe
Not exactly the boy next door

THE VALLEY OF UNREST

Electronic music

LIGEIA
Far away, far away,
Are not all lovely things far away?
As far at least lies that valley as the bedridden
Sun in the luminous east,
The paralyzed mountains, the sickly river.
Are not all things lovely far away?
Are not all things lovely far away?

It is a valley where time is not interrupted,
Where its history shall not be interpreted.
Stories of Satan's dart—
Of angel wings—
Unhappy things
Within the valley of unrest.

The sun ray dripped all red,
The dell was silent—
All the people having gone to war
Leaving no interrogator to mind the willful
Looting, the pale past knowledge,
The sly mysterious stars,

The unguarded flowers leaning,
The tulips overhead paler,
The terror-stricken sky
Rolling like a waterfall
Over the horizon's fiery wall—
A visage full of meaning.

How the unhappy shall confess
As Roderick watches like a human eye
While the violets and lilies wave
Like banners in the sky hovering
Over and above a grave
As dewdrops on the freshly planted
Eternal dew coming down in gems.
There's no use to pretend
Though gorgeous clouds fly,
Roderick like the human eye has closed forever
Far away far away.

Roderick, whatever thy image may be
Roderick, no magic shall sever the music from thee,
Thou hast bound many eyes in a dreamy sleep.
O tortured day the strains still arrive—
I hear the bells—I have kept my vigilance.

Rain dancing in the rhythm of a shower
Over what guilty spirit to not hear the beating,
To not hear the beating heart
But only tears of perfect moan,
Only tears of perfect moan.

CALL ON ME

ROWENA
Caught in the crossbow of ideas and journeys
Sit here reliving the other self's mournings
Caught in the crossbow of ideas and dawnings
Stand I

Reliving the past of the maddening impulse
The violent upheaval
The pure driven instinct
The pure driven murder
The attraction of daring
Stand I

Why didn't you call on me
Why didn't you call on me
Why didn't you call on me
Why didn't you call

A wild being from birth
My spirit spurns control
Wandering the wide earth
Searching for my soul
Dimly peering
I would surely find

What could there be more purely bright
than truth's daystar

Why didn't you call on me
Why didn't you call on me
Why didn't you call on me
Why didn't you call

Why didn't you call on me
Why didn't you call on me
Why didn't you call on me
Why didn't you call

THE CITY IN THE SEA

Electronic music, soft

OLD POE
Death has reared himself a throne.

YOUNG POE
In a strange city—alone.

LENORE
Death has reared himself a throne
In a strange city—alone.
Their shrines and palaces are not like ours,
They do not tremble and rot,
Eaten with time.

OLD POE
Death has reared himself a throne.

LENORE
Lifted by forgotten winds
Resignedly beneath the sky
The melancholy waters lie
A crown of stars.

YOUNG POE
In a strange city—alone.

LENORE
A heaven God does not condemn.
But the everlasting shadow
Makes mockery of it all.

ROWENA
No holy rays come down.
Lights from the lurid deep sea stream up the
Turrets silently,
Up thrones, up arbors
Of sculpted ivy and stone flowers,
Up domes, up spires.
Kingly halls all are melancholy shrines,
The columns, frieze, and entablature
Chokingly shockingly intertwined,
The mast, the viol, and the vine
Twisted.

YOUNG POE
There amid no earthly moans
Hell rises from a thousand thrones.

OLD POE
Does reverence to death.

OLD POE AND YOUNG POE
And death does give his undivided time.

LIGEIA
There are open temples and graves
On a level with the waves.
Death looms and looks—huge!—gigantic!
There is a ripple—now a wave
Towers thrown aside
Sinking in the dull tide
The waves growing redder
The very hours losing their breath.

POE
Oh, the cunning stars watching fitfully over night after night
of matchless wretched sleep—matched only with the horror
of the dream unfolding—the telltale beating of the heart—
the suffocating breath—the desire—the pose—one poses upon
the precipice—to fall to run to dive to tumble to fall down
down into the spiral down and then. . . .

OLD POE

One sees one's own death—one sees one committing murder or atrocious violent acts—and then a cursed shadow not of man or God but a shadow resting upon a brazen doorway.

YOUNG POE

There were seven of us there who saw the shadow as it came out from among the draperies. But we did not dare behold it. We looked down into the depths of the mirror of ebony. And the apparition spoke.

Electronic reverberation added to voice

"I am a shadow and I dwell in the catacombs which border the country of illusion hard by the dim plains of wishing."

OLD POE

And then did we start shuddering, starting from our seats trembling—for the tones in the voice of the shadow were not the tones of any one man but of a multitude of beings and, varying in their cadences from syllable to syllable, fell duskily upon our ears in the well-remembered and familiar accents of a thousand departed friends.

Instrumental track: "A Thousand Departed Friends"

CHANGE

Death
The only thing constantly changing is change
And change is always for the worse
The worm on the hook always eaten by a fish
The fish by a bird man or worse
A spot on the lung a spot on your heart
An aneurysm of the soul
The only thing constantly changing is change
And it comes equipped with a curse

The only thing constantly changing is change
And it's always for the worse
The only thing constantly changing is change
And it's always for the worse

The only thing constantly changing is change
The living only become dead
Your hair falling out
Your liver swelled up
Your teeth rot your gums and your chin
Your ass starts to sag
Your balls shrivel up
Your cock swallowed up in its sack

The only thing constantly changing is change
And it's always change on your back.

The only thing constantly changing is change
And it's always for the worse
The only thing constantly changing is change
And it's always for the worse

The only thing constantly changing is change
Ashes to ashes to dust
The deer and the rabbit
The musk of your hole
Filled up with myriad dread
The dread of the living
The dread of the living
The frightening pulse of the night.
The only thing constantly changing is change.
Its changes will kill us with fright

The only thing constantly changing is change
And it's always for the worse
The only thing constantly changing is change
And it's always for the worse

The only thing constantly changing is change
The only thing constantly changing is change
The only thing constantly changing is change
And it comes equipped with my curse

THE FALL OF THE HOUSE OF USHER

POE
And then I had a vision.

The sound of knocking on a door, the door opening, a storm in the background

RODERICK USHER
Ah Edgar, ah Edgar, my dear friend Edgar.

POE
It's been a long time, Roderick. I've ridden many miles. It's been a dull and soundless day for autumn. The leaves have lost their autumn glow, and the clouds seem oppressive with their drifting finery.

USHER
I know, my friend. Though I own so much of this land I find the country insufferable. I deal only in half pleasures.

POE
Speaking of half pleasures, would you care for a tincture of opium?

USHER

Nothing would please me more than to smoke with an old friend.

The sound of a match being struck, inhalation of smoke

USHER

I have experienced the hideous dropping of the veil, the bitter lapse into common life, unredeemed dreariness of thought. I have an iciness, a sickening of the heart.

Long pause

POE

It's true you don't look well, Roderick, but I am your friend no matter the occasion or position of the stars. I'm glad you wrote me, but I must admit to concern.

The sound of rain

USHER

I cannot contain my heart. Edgar, I look to you for solace, for relief from myself. What I have is constitutional, a family evil, a nervous affection that must surely pass. But I do have this morbid acuteness of senses. I can eat only the most insipid food, clothes only of the lightest texture. The odor of flowers I find oppressive. My eyes cannot bear even the faintest light.

A soft moaning
Did you hear that?

POE
I hear. I am listening—go on.

USHER
I shall perish. I will perish in this deplorable folly. I dread the future. Not the events, the results. The most trivial event causes the greatest agitation of the soul. I do not fear danger except in its absolute effect—terror. I find I must inevitably abandon life and reason together, in my struggles with the demon fear.

Sound of strong wind
Perhaps you'll think me superstitious, but the *physique* of this place; it hovers about me like a great body, some diseased outer shell, some decaying finite skin encasing my morale.

POE

You mentioned your sister was ill.

USHER

My beloved sister, my sole companion, has had a long continuing illness whose inevitable conclusion seems forsworn. This will leave me the last of the ancient race of Ushers.

Soft moaning

POE

She looks so much like you.

USHER

I love her in a nameless way, more than I love myself. Her demise will leave me hopelessly confined to memories and realities of a future so barren as to be stultifying.

Moaning continues

POE

What of physicians?

Usher

They are baffled. Until today she refused bed rest, wanting to be present in your honor, but finally she succumbed to the prostrating power of the destroyer. You will probably see her no more.

Guitar melody begins

Poe

Sound and music take us to the twin curves of experience. Like brother and sister intertwined, they relieve themselves of bodily contact and dance in a pagan revelry.

Usher

I have soiled myself with my designs. I am ashamed of my brain. The enemy is me and the executioner terror.

Music is a reflection of our inner self; unfiltered agony touches the wayward string. The wayward brain confuses itself with the self-perceived future and turns inward with loathing and terror. Either by design or thought we are doomed to know our own end.

I have written a lyric.

Poe

May I hear it?

USHER
It is called "The Haunted Palace."

In the greenest of our valleys
By good angels tenanted,
Once a fair and stately palace—
Snow-white palace—reared its head.

Banners yellow, glorious, golden,
On its roof did float and flow—
(This—all this—was in the olden
Time long ago)

The sound of thunder
And every gentle air that dallied,
Along the rampart plumed and pallid,
A winged odor went away.

All wanderers in that happy valley
Through two luminous windows saw
Spirits moving musically
The sovereign of the realm serene,
A troop of echoes whose sweet duty
Was but to sing

In voices of surpassing beauty
The wit and wisdom of the king.

But evil things, in robes of sorrow,
Assailed the monarch's high estate.
And round about his home the glory
Is but a dim remembered story.

Vast forms that move fantastically
To a discordant melody,
While like a ghastly river
A hideous throng rush out forever
And laugh—but smile no more—
Nevermore.

POE
It's cold in here.

USHER
I tell you minerals are sentient things. The gradual yet certain
condensation of an atmosphere of their own about the waters
and the walls proves this. Thus the silent yet importunate and
terrible influence which for centuries has molded my family.

And now me.

A scream

USHER
Excuse me!

Chaotic sounds
She is gone. Out, sad light, Roderick has no life.

Soft sounds of creaking and rustling
I shall preserve her corpse for a fortnight.

POE
But Roderick—

USHER
I shall place it in a vault facing the lake. I do not wish to
answer to the medical men nor place her in the exposed burial
plot of my family. We shall inter her at the proper date when
I am more fully of a right mind. . . . Her malady was unusual.
   Please do not question me on this.

POE
I cannot question you.

USHER

Then help me now.

Sound of coffin opening

POE

One would think you twins.

USHER

We are. We have always been sympathetic to each other. . . .
Have you seen this? It is her!

Swirling electronic sounds

POE

It is a whirlwind! You should not—you must not behold this!

Slamming of coffin

Roderick, these appearances, which bewilder you are mere
electrical phenomena, not uncommon. Or perhaps they have
their rank origins in the marshy gases of the lake. Please, let's
close this casement and I will read and you will listen and
together we will pass this terrible night together. . . . What's
that?

Sound of metal clanging and muffled reverberation
What's that? Don't you hear that?

USHER

Not hear it? Yes, I hear it and have heard it—many minutes—have I heard it? Oh, pity me miserable wretch: I dared not—oh, no—I dared not speak! We have put her living in the tomb. I have heard feeble movements in the coffin—I thought I heard—I dared not speak.

Sounds of a storm and many people screaming
Oh, God, I have heard footsteps—do you not hear them?—attention. Do I not distinguish that heavy and horrible beating of her heart? Madman, madman! I tell you she now stands without the door!

Sounds of fire and screams, a loud heartbeat

THE BED

LADY MADELINE OF USHER
This is the place where she laid her head
When she went to bed at night
And this is the place our children were conceived
Candles lit the room at night

And this is the place where she cut her wrists
That odd and fateful night
And I said, Oh, oh, oh, oh, oh, oh, what a feeling
And I said, Oh, oh, oh, oh, oh, oh, what a feeling

This is the place where we used to live
I paid for it with love and blood
And these are the boxes that she kept on the shelf
Filled with her poetry and stuff

And this is the room where she took the razor
And cut her wrists that strange and fateful night
And I said, Oh, oh, oh, oh, oh, oh, what a feeling
And I said, Oh, oh, oh, oh, oh, oh, what a feeling

I never would have started if I'd known
That it'd end this way
But funny thing I'm not at all sad
That it stopped this way
Stopped this way

PERFECT DAY

LENORE
Just a perfect day
Drink sangria in the park
And then later when it gets dark
We go home
Just a perfect day
Feed animals in the zoo
Then later a movie too
And then home

Oh it's such a perfect day
I'm glad I spent it with you
Oh such a perfect day
You just keep me hangin' on
You just keep me hangin' on

Just a perfect day
Problems all left alone
Weekenders on our own
It's such fun
Just a perfect day
You make me forget myself
I thought I was someone else
Someone good

Oh it's such a perfect day
I'm glad I spent it with you
Oh such a perfect day
You just keep me hangin' on
You just keep me hangin' on

THE RAVEN

Soft cello and electronics

POE

1.

Once upon a midnight dreary, as I pondered, weak and
    weary,
Over many a quaint and curious volume of forgotten lore—
While I nodded, nearly napping, suddenly there came a
    tapping,
As of someone gently rapping, rapping at my chamber door.
"'Tis some visitor," I muttered, "tapping at my chamber
    door—
                Only this and nothing more."

2.

Muttering I got up weakly (always I've had trouble sleeping),
Stumbling upright, my mind racing, furtive thoughts
    flowing once more
I there hoping for some sunrise happiness would be a
    surprise
Loneliness no longer a prize rapping at my chamber door
Seeking out the clever bore lost in dreams for evermore—
                Only this and nothing more.

3.

Hovering, my pulse was racing, stale tobacco my lips tasting,
Scotch sitting upon my basin, remnants of the night before.
Came again infernal tapping on the door, in my mind
    jabbing—
Is it in or outside rapping? calling out to me once more
The fit and fury of Lenore

        Nameless *here* for evermore.

4.

And the silken, sad, uncertain rustling of the purple curtain
Thrilled me—filled me with fantastic terrors never felt
    before;
So that now (O wind!) stop breathing, hoping yet to calm
    my breathing
"'Tis some visitor entreating entrance at my chamber door—
Some lost visitor entreating entrance at my chamber door—

        This it is and nothing more."

5.

Deep into the darkness peering, long I stood there
    wondering, fearing,
Doubting, dreaming fantasies no mortal dared to dream
    before,

But the silence was unbroken and the stillness gave no token,
And the only word there spoken was the whispered name,
    "Lenore?"
This I thought and out loud whispered, from my lips the
    foul name festered—echoing itself
          Merely this and nothing more.

6.

Back into my chamber turning, every nerve within me
    burning,
When once again I heard a tapping somewhat louder than
    before,
"Surely," said I, "surely that is something at my iron staircase;
Open the door to see what 'threat' is—open the window,
Free the shutters—let us this mystery explore—
O bursting heart be still this once! And let this mystery
    explore—
          It is the wind and nothing more."

7.

Just one epithet I muttered as inside I gagged and shuddered
    with manly flirt and flutter
In there flew a stately Raven, Sleek and ravenous as any foe.
Not the least obeisance made he—not a minute's gesture
    toward me

Of recognition or politeness—but perched above my
    chamber door—
This fowl and salivating visage insinuating with its
    knowledge—
Perched above my chamber door
            Silent sat and staring nothing more.

8.

Askance! Askew! The self's sad fancy smiles,
I swear, at this savage vicious countenance it wears
"Though you show here shorn and shaven, and I admit
    myself forlorn and craven
Ghastly grim and ancient Raven wandering from the opiate
    shores
Tell me what thy lordly name is, that you are not nightmare
    sewage,
Some dire powder drink or inhalation framed from flames
    of downtown lore"—
            Quoth the Raven, "Nevermore."

9.

And the Raven, sitting lonely, staring sickly at my male sex
    only,
That one word, as if his soul in that one word he did outpour.

Pathetic!!!

Nothing further then he uttered, not a feather then he
    fluttered—

Till finally was I that muttered as I stared dully at the floor,

"Other friends have flown and left me, flown as each and
    every hope has flown before

As you no doubt will 'fore the morrow"—

    But the bird said, "Never. More."

10.

Then I felt the air grow denser, perfumed from some
    unseen incense

As though accepting angelic intrusion (when in fact I felt
    collusion)

Before the guise of false memories respite! Respite through
    the haze of cocaine's glory

I smoke and smoke the blue vial's glory to forget—at
    once!!!—the base Lenore—

    Quoth the Raven, "Nevermore."

11.

"Prophet!" said I, "thing of evil!—prophet still, if bird or devil!—

By that heaven that bends above us—by that God we both
    ignore—

Tell this soul with sorrow laden willful and destructive
    intent
How had lapsed a pure heart lady to the greediest of needs
Sweaty arrogant dickless liar who ascribed to nothing
    higher
Than a jab from prick to needle
Straight to betrayal and disgrace?
The conscience showing not a trace—
            Quoth the Raven, "Nevermore."

12.

"Be that word our sign of parting, bird or fiend!" I yelled,
    upstarting—
"Get thee back into the tempest into the smoke-filled
    bottle's shore!
Leave no black plume as a token of the slime thy soul has
    spoken!
Leave my loneliness unbroken!—quit as those have quit
    before!
Take the talon from my heart and see that I can care no
    more."
Whatever mattered came before I vanished with the dead
    Lenore!"
            Quoth the Raven, "Nevermore."

13.

But the Raven, never flitting, still is sitting, silent sitting,

Above a painting silent painting of the forever silenced
whore,

And his eyes have all the seeming of a demon that is
dreaming,

And the lamplight o'er him streaming throws his shadow to
the floor.

I love she who hates me more! I love she who hates me
more!

And my soul shall not be lifted from that shadow.
Nevermore!

BALLOON

ENTERTAINER

I'm a little balloon and I get puffed up
Squeeze me and bend me it's never enough
Put your lips around me, blow me up
But if you prick me I will pop

I'm a little balloon full and firm
Here's my aft and here's my stern
Here's my lips and here's my hose
Put me down or I will burst
If you prick me I will burst!

ACT II

Generic lounge music with walking bass

ENTERTAINER

I'd like to thank all you people for showing up tonight. Sorry about the weather—Let's have a big hand for my longtime accompanist Manfred Gooseberry—hey, Goose, take a bow, relax, be comfortable, have a cocktail in the Poo Poo Lounge—and let us entertain you.

BROADWAY SONG

I'd like to sing you a Broadway song
I hope that you'll all sing along
A little dancing and some sentiment to put your
Mind at ease

I'd like to play you something low and sexy
Look at our dancers they're so young and pretty—hi Olga!
And when we start to groove you can hear the
Saxophones blow

Ah show business is just a wonderful thing
All I want is to get down on my knees and sing
For you
And let the saxophones blow
Blow baby blow

I'd like to sing you a Broadway song
I hope that you'll all sing along
A little dancing and some sentiment to put your
Mind at ease

I wanna bring a tear to your eye
Awww good old Poe don't he make you cry

Ain't it great the way he writes about the
Mysteries of life

Ah show business is just a wonderful thing
All I want is to get down on my knees and sing
For you
And let the saxophones blow
Blow baby blow
Go goose go

THE TELLTALE HEART, PART 1

*Electronics with feedback; voices in Ensemble placed spatially
with various amounts of reverb*

OLD POE
True! Nervous, very nervous.

POE 1
Madman!

YOUNG POE
Why will you say that I am mad? The disease has sharpened
my senses—not destroyed—not dulled them.

POE 2
Madman!

POE 3
The eye of a vulture—a pale blue eye, with a film over it.

OLD POE
Listen! Observe how healthily and how calmly I tell this story.

POE 5
He had no passion for the old man. He was never insulted.

POE 4
He loved him.

POE 1
It was the eye the eye the eye.

YOUNG POE
I made up my mind. To take his life forever.

POE 2
Passionless.

POE 3
The eye of a vulture.

YOUNG POE
You should have seen me.

POE 5
You should have seen him.

OLD POE
How wisely I proceeded.

POE 4
To rid himself of the eye forever.

YOUNG POE
With what dissimulation I went to work!

ALL
Caution!

OLD POE
I turned the latch on his door and opened it.

POE 1
To work.

POE 2
To practice.

YOUNG POE
I opened his door and put in a dark lantern.

ALL
Dark.

OLD POE

Slowly I put my head in; slowly I thrust it until in time I entered. I was in so far. . . .

Feedback swelling

POE 3

He was in so far he could see the old man sleep.

OLD POE

And then I undid the lantern so a thin ray fell upon the eye.

POE 5

The vulture eye.

POE 4

He did this for seven days.

POE 1

Seven days.

YOUNG POE

But always the eye was closed, and so I could not do the work.

POE 2

And in the day he would greet the old man calmly in his chamber.

POE 3

Calmly.

OLD POE

Nothing is wrong and all is well.

POE 5

Knock, knock—who's there?

POE 4

Came night eight.

ALL

Night eight.

YOUNG POE

I was slower than a watch minute hand. The power that I had with the old man not to even dream my secret thoughts.

POE 1
Secret thoughts.

OLD POE
My sagacity. I could barely conceal my feelings of triumph.

YOUNG POE
When suddenly the body moved.

POE 2
The body moved.

OLD POE
But I went in even further, pushing the door open even further.

POE 3
"Who's there?"

ALL
"Who's there?"

YOUNG POE
I did not move a muscle. I kept quiet and still.

POE 5
The old man sat up in bed.

POE 4
In his bed.

ALL
"Who's there?"

OLD POE
I heard a groan and knew it was a groan of mortal terror, not pain or grief.

ALL
Oh, no!

YOUNG POE
It was the low stifled sound that arises from the bottom of the soul when overcharged with awe. I felt such awe welling up in my own bosom, deepening with its echo the terrors that distracted me. Knowing what the old man felt and—

POE 1
—pitying him—

POE 2
—pitying him.

YOUNG POE
Although it made me laugh.

ALL
Ha-ha!

OLD POE
He'd been lying awake since the first slight noise. He'd been lying awake thinking . . .

POE 3
. . . thinking . . .

POE 5
. . . it is nothing but the wind.

POE 4
The wind.

POE 1
It is nothing but the house settling.

POE 2
The old man stalked with his black shadow.

POE 3
Death approaching.

OLD POE
The mournful presence of the unperceived causing him to
feel my presence.

POE 5
Open the lantern!

YOUNG POE
I saw the ray fall on the eye.

ALL
On the eye.

BLIND RAGE

THE OLD MAN

Who's that peeping through my door
Sneaking up and down the hall
I can't stand it anymore
I can't stand it anymore
Who's that peeping through my door
Sneaking up and down the hall
I can't stand it anymore
I can't stand it anymore
Blind rage . . . I'm in a blind rage
Blind rage
Blind rage
Blind rage

Who's that creeping in my room
Blocking out the stars and moon
I fear you will attack me soon
Who goes there!!!

Who's that creeping in my room
Blocking out the stars and moon
I fear you will attack me soon
Who goes there!!!

Blind rage
Blind rage

Blind rage
Blind rage
I'm in a blind rage

Blind rage you're making me scared
You're making me scared
Blind rage

Blind rage
Blind rage
Blind rage

Blind rage
Blind rage
I'm in a blind rage

THE TELLTALE HEART, PART 2

Organ and electronics

POE 4
Furious!

OLD POE
It made me furious!

POE 1
A dull quick sound, pounding.

POE 2
Like a watch encased in cotton.

ALL
Tick-tock.

OLD POE
I knew that sound well.

YOUNG POE
It increased my fury.

POE 3
The beating of the old man's heart.

OLD POE
I scarcely breathed and refrained.

YOUNG POE
Motionless.

POE 5
The tattoo of the heart—

POE 4
Hellish—

POE 1
Increased and was extreme.

POE 2
It grew louder.

POE 3
Louder.

OLD POE

I am nervous at this dead hour of the night; amid the dreadful silence of this old house, this sound excites me to uncontrollable wrath. I thought someone would hear this sound, I thought his heart would burst.

YOUNG POE

His hour had come.

Loud metallic knocking
Open the door!

Loud metallic knocking; enter Policemen

POLICEMAN I

Police, open the door.

YOUNG POE

The old man has gone to the country.

POLICEMAN I

Gone to the country.

OLD POE
But please search well.

POLICEMAN 2
Please search well.

YOUNG POE
These are his treasures.

POLICEMAN 3
Treasures.

YOUNG POE
Secure and undisturbed.

OLD POE
Please sit and rest. You must be fatigued.

YOUNG POE
Wild audacity. Perfect triumph.

POLICEMAN 1
So they chat.

ALL
Chat.

POLICEMAN 3
Of familiar things.

YOUNG POE
I hear ringing.

OLD POE
Ringing.

YOUNG POE
Do you not hear it?

POLICEMEN
No.

OLD POE
It is louder. It is making my head ache. Do you not hear it?

POLICEMAN 1
No.

POLICEMAN 2
No.

POLICEMAN 3
No.

YOUNG POE
I—I have a headache.

Knocking continues
The day is long. Do you not hear it?

POLICEMEN
No!

OLD POE
Do you fucking mock me? Do you mock me?

YOUNG POE
They know!

OLD POE
Do you think me—

YOUNG POE
They know!

Knocking stops

OLD POE
—an imbecile? Do you think me a fool! Villains, dissemble no more!

OLD POE AND YOUNG POE
I admit the deed!

YOUNG POE
Admit! Admit!

OLD POE
Here, here!

OLD POE AND YOUNG POE
Admit!

OLD POE
It is the beating of his most hideous heart!

BURNING EMBERS

POLICEMEN
Fly through the glass of a windowpane
Fall through the sky feeling the rain
Walk on broken glass your telltale heart

Look through the bars of a dirty jail cell
Soar to heaven dive to hell
Listen to your telltale heart

Setting fires in the ghost twilight
We see you dress we bolt with fright
You see an apparition disappear

Ah . . . jump to the table jump up the stairs
Stand on the rooftop looking out through the air
Walk on broken glass your telltale heart

Lenore am I dreaming
How can death keep us apart
Lenore I see you burning. . . .
And I'd walk on burning embers
Walk on burning embers
Walk on burning embers telltale heart

Walk on burning embers
Walk on burning embers
Walk on burning embers
Telltale heart

THE IMP OF THE PERVERSE

Rhythmic electronics

FEMALE TEACHER
Death by a visitation from God. Death by a visitation from God.

MALE STUDENT
I am shadow.

FEMALE TEACHER
Things material and spiritual . . .

MALE STUDENT
Maternal.

FEMALE TEACHER
. . . can be heavy.

MALE STUDENT
Suffocating.

FEMALE TEACHER
There are seven iron lamps which illumine our senses.

MALE STUDENT
Seven knives.

FEMALE TEACHER
Seven iron lamps to illumine our senses and seven bells to celebrate the resurrection.

MALE STUDENT
Two marble balls in a sack. One long and slender candle. One mouth, two reckonings. Consternation and treachery.

FEMALE TEACHER
Are you listening? *Are you listening to me?* Are you paying attention? *To me!*

MALE STUDENT
I am shadow.

FEMALE TEACHER
Seven iron lamps, seven oboes, two small balls, and one tiny candle.

MALE STUDENT
Tiny candle.

FEMALE TEACHER
One pathetic flame, embers dying.

MALE STUDENT
Dying.

FEMALE TEACHER
Five creatures from the monolith, seven whispers from the
catacombs, five and seven numbing mumbling speeches—are
you listening?

MALE STUDENT
I am drawn to do what I should not!

FEMALE TEACHER
Guilty guilty guilty guilty no no never never no; seven morn-
ings, thirteen moons, five wolves, one silk-spread morning,
seven bells for seven senses each one lusting lusting.

MALE STUDENT
Guiltily.

FEMALE TEACHER

Two milk-fed glands ripe and red-tipped—are you listening, my little mouse? Each sense ripped from its bodice, each gland primed to its overflow—do you hear me, my little mouse man, do you hear me, little cock?

MALE STUDENT

Semen!

FEMALE TEACHER

Are you listening, my little tumescent smear?

MALE STUDENT

Ligeia! I stand on the edge and am drawn to it! Guilt! I am shadow!

Music swells, becomes louder

VANISHING ACT

TEACHER AND STUDENT

It must be nice to disappear
To have a vanishing act
To always be looking forward
And never looking back

How nice it is to disappear
Float into a mist
With a young lady on your arm
Looking for a kiss

It might be nice to disappear
To have a vanishing act
To always be looking forward
Never look over your back

It must be nice to disappear
Float into a mist
With a young lady on your arm
Looking for a kiss

THE CASK

Young Poe

Never bet the Devil your head. When I was an infant my mother treated me like a tough steak. To her well-regulated mind, babies were the better for beatings. But she was left-handed, and a child flogged left-handed is better left unflogged.

The world revolves from right to left. It will not do to whip a baby from left to right. If each blow in the right direction drives an evil propensity out, a blow in the opposite direction knocks its quota of wickedness in.

Hence my precocity in vice, my sensitivity to injuries, the thousands of injuries heaped upon me by Fortunato, and then finally his rabid insults, for which I vowed revenge.

I gave no utterance to threat. But the knowledge of "avengemanship" was so definite, so precise, that no risk could befall me; by neither word nor deed had I given cause to doubt my goodwill. I would punish with impunity. I will fuck him up the ass and piss in his face. I will redress the wrong.

But lips and psyche, mind, be silent. Fortunato approaches.

THE CASK

Fortunato
Don't take me to task
For loving a cask
The cask of Amontillado

Please don't make a pass
You can go kiss my ass
All I want is this mythical cask
The cask of Amontillado

I've heard so much through the grapevine
I've heard so much on the line
But the one thing that I lust after
Is the one thing I've never had

So is it too much to ask
To have just one taste of the cask
Why you could go kiss my ass
For the cask of Amontillado

Edgar, old fellow, dear bosom friend. Hail fellow well met. O great elucidator, great epopee.

YOUNG POE

Ah, Fortunato, what luck to meet you, what good luck to meet you and see you looking so splendid. I have received a cask of Amontillado—or what passes for Amontillado.

FORTUNATO

Amontillado? That most wondrous sherry? A cask? Impossible! How? So rare.

YOUNG POE

I've had my doubts. I was silly enough to pay the full price without consulting you in the matter, but you were not to be found and I was fearful of losing a bargain.

FORTUNATO

Fearfully stupid if you ask me, Edgar.

YOUNG POE

I am on my way to see Mr. Bolo—

FORTUNATO

A cask.

YOUNG POE
A cask. To gather his opinion. Are you engaged?

FORTUNATO
Mr. Bolo cannot tell Amontillado from goat's milk.

YOUNG POE
Yet some say his taste is a match for your own.

FORTUNATO
Hardly, dear boy. Let us go.

YOUNG POE
Where?

FORTUNATO
To your vaults . . . to the supposed Amontillado.

YOUNG POE
Oh, my good friend, no. I could not impose upon your good
nature. You have, after all, an engagement.

FORTUNATO

To hell with the engagement. I have no engagement. Before the sky withers and falls, let us go.

YOUNG POE

But the vaults are damp and I see you are afflicted with a severe cold.

FORTUNATO

Let us go! The cold is nothing. You've been taken advantage of. And Mr. Bolo cannot tell Amontillado from piss. The cask?

YOUNG POE

It is farther on. But see the white webwork which gleams from the cavern walls.

FORTUNATO

Nitre? Nitre?

YOUNG POE

How long have you had that cough? Yes, nitre.

FORTUNATO

It is nothing.

YOUNG POE

We should go back. Your health is precious. You are a man who would be missed. Let's return. I cannot be responsible for causing you ill health. And anyway, there's always Mr. Bolo.

FORTUNATO

Be damned! I'll not be swayed. The cough is nothing. It will not kill me. I won't die of a cough.

YOUNG POE

Of that you can be sure. Have some of this Médoc to warm the bones and defend you from this infernal dampness. Drink. Drink, damn you.

FORTUNATO

I drink to the buried that repose around us.

YOUNG POE

And I to your long life.

The nitre. It hangs like moss. We are below the river's bed. The moisture trickles and chills the bones. Let's go back. Your cough.

FORTUNATO

The cough is nothing! Let us have some more Médoc. . . .
Let us proceed to the Amontillado.

YOUNG POE

So, proceed. Herein the Amontillado. Now, Mr. Bolo—

FORTUNATO

Mr. Bolo is an imbecile! An ignoramus.

YOUNG POE

Can you not feel the nitre? You really should go. I implore
you. No? Then I must leave you here. But first let me render
you all the little attentions within my power.

FORTUNATO

The Amontillado. Ha, ha, ha. A very good joke indeed. We will
have many a rich laugh about it over our wine in the palazzo.

YOUNG POE

The Amontillado!

FORTUNATO

Yes yes yes. The Amontillado.

YOUNG POE
Well, then, let's go!

Feedback

FORTUNATO
For the love of God!

YOUNG POE
Precisely for the love of God. Fortunato! Fortunato!

Feedback continues and grows louder

GUILTY

Electronics and guitar drones

MOTHER
Guilty?

DAUGHTER
Guilty.

MOTHER
I'm paralyzed with guilt,
It runs through me like rain through silk.
Guilty? My mind won't leave me alone.
My teeth are rotten, my lips start to foam
'Cause I'm so guilty.

DAUGHTER
Guilty, guilty.

MOTHER
Ohhhhh—guilty!
What did I say? What did I do?
Did I ever do it to you?
Don't turn your back!
I can't look you in the eyeeyeeye.

DAUGHTER
Eyeeyeeye.

MOTHER
I guess I am guilty as charged.

DAUGHTER
Guilty, guilty, guilty, guilty,
Guilty, guilty, guilty, guilty, guilty.

MOTHER
Don't do that.

DAUGHTER
Don't do what?

MOTHER
Don't—do—that!
Oh, you're such a child!
Guilty—what can I do?
I do it to you
But I do it to me too.
Cut off my head—hang me from the yardarm.
Guilty? I'm paralyzed with guilt,

I've got bad thoughts,
I've got an evil clit.

MOTHER
Guilty.

MOTHER
My mind won't leave me alone,
I've got a bad mind, I've got a bad bone.

DAUGHTER
Guilty—guilty as charged—guilty.

MOTHER
Don't do that.

DAUGHTER
Don't do what?

MOTHER
Don't—do—that!
Oh, you're such a reckless child!
You remember when you were a baby?

MOTHER
Do you have a jury?

DAUGHTER
Yeah.

MOTHER
Do they have a verdict?

DAUGHTER
Guilty as charged.

DAUGHTER
Guilty, guilty,
Guilty as charged.

MOTHER
Do they have a verdict?
Do they have a verdict!
I'm guilty!

DAUGHTER
You're guilty.

MOTHER

Oh, you are such a reckless child!
I should beat you.
I should hit you!
I will put you in therapy.

DAUGHTER

Guilty, guilty,
Guilty, guilty.

MOTHER (LAUGHING)

Guilty.

Dialogue to be sung

A WILD BEING FROM BIRTH

Electronics and organ

ROWENA

A wild being from birth
My spirit spurns control,
Wandering the wide earth
Searching for my soul.

While all the world is chiding
In visions of the dark night
I have had a waking dream,
A holy dream a holy dream.

A waking dream of life and light
That cheered me as a lovely beam,
A lonely spirit guiding
With a ray turned back upon the past.

While I aghast
Sit motionless through the misty night
Dimly peering at what once shone bright
Peeking wariy at what shone afar—
What could there be more purely bright
In truth's daystar?

Ligeia

In the consideration of the faculties and impulses of the human soul in consideration of our arrogance, our radical, primitive, irreducible arrogance of reason, we have all overlooked the propensity. We saw no need for it the paradoxical something which we may call perverseness. A *mobile* without motive. Through its promptings, we act without comprehensible object. Induction would have brought phrenology to admit this. We act for the reason we should not. For certain minds this is absolutely irresistible. The conviction of the wrong or impolicy of an action is often the unconquerable force. It is a primitive impulse.

Elementary—the overwhelming tendency to do wrong for the wrong's sake. This impels us to its persecutions. O holy dream. We persist in acts because we feel that we should *not* persist in them. This is the combativeness of phrenology.

Rowena

We have a task before us which must be speedily performed. We know it will be ruinous to delay. Trumpet-tongued, the important crisis of our life calls. We glow.

Ligeia

We are consumed with eagerness to commence work. Yet a shadow flits across the brain. The impulse increases to a wish, the wish to a desire, the desire to uncontrollable longing, and the longing in defiance of all consequences is indulged. We put off all until tomorrow.

ROWENA

We tremble with the violence of the conflict within us—the definite with the indefinite, the substance with the shadow.

There is no answer except that we feel perverse. The shadow prevails. Our energy returns. We will commit now, we will labor now—O holiest of dreams—but it is too late. We stand upon the brink of the precipice.

LIGEIA

We grow sick and dizzy. We go to shrink from danger but instead we approach it. We are intoxicated by the mere idea of a fall from such a great height. This fall, this rushing annihilation—for the very reason it contains the most loathsome and ghastly images of death and suffering—for this reason do we now most impetuously desire it. There is no passion in nature so demonic as the passion of him who, shuddering upon the edge, meditates a plunge. We will these actions merely because we feel that we should not. Having realized this, I swoon. It is the spirit of the perverse. The idea of a poison candle struck my fancy, and I procured one for my victim. I will not vex you with impertinent details, but suffice it to say the verdict was "Death by the visitation of God."

ROWENA

All went well for me.

LIGEIA

All went well for me.

ROWENA

His estate inherited, I reveled in absolute security. I would never be found out. I was safe. I was safe—if I did not prove fool enough to make open confession.

LIGEIA

If I did not prove fool enough to make public confession. No sooner had I uttered those words than I felt an icy chill creep into my heart. I made a strong effort to shake off this nightmare of the soul. I laughed. I whistled. I walked and then walked faster. I thought I saw a formless shape approaching me from behind. And then I ran. I pushed and shoved blindly. I thought I felt a hand upon my throat—no mortal hand. I screamed, and then clearly, clearly, I enunciated pregnant sentences that consigned me to the hangman and to hell, the fullest judicial conviction.

Today I wear chains but tomorrow I shall be fetterless. But where?

O holy dream, O beam of light, I fall prostrate with excitement this holy night.

I WANNA KNOW (PIT AND PENDULUM)

YOUNG POE

Under the intense scrutiny of Ligeia's eyes, I have felt the full knowledge and force of their expression and yet have been unable to possess it and have felt it leave me as so many other things have left—the letter half-read, the bottle half-drunk—finding in the commonest objects of the universe a circle of analogies, of metaphors for that expression which has been willfully withheld from me, the access to the inner soul denied.

JUDGES AND DEAD PEOPLE (CHOIR)

I wanna know.

YOUNG POE

In consideration of the faculties and impulses of the human soul in consideration of our arrogance, our radical, primitive, irreducible arrogance of reason, we have all overlooked the propensity. We saw no need for it, the paradoxical something which we may call perverseness. Through its promptings, we act without comprehensible object.

We act for the reason we should not. For certain minds this is absolutely irresistible. The conviction of the wrong or impolicy of an action is often the unconquerable force. It is a primitive impulse. The overwhelming tendency to do wrong for the wrong's sake. We persist in acts because we feel that we should *not* persist in them.

JUDGES AND DEAD PEOPLE (CHOIR)
I wanna know.

SCIENCE OF THE MIND

YOUNG POE
In the science of the mind
There is no forgiving
Paralyzed I lay here sleeping
Quiet as a little child
Heart starts beating
Blood rushing pounding
Moving quiet as a little lamb

In the science of the mind
Limbs are bound devoid of movement
The injuries we do in kind
Are visited upon us often

In the science of the mind
Trying hard to move a shadow
Don't bury me I'm still alive
The science of the mind unyielding
The science of the mind unyielding
The science of the mind unyielding

ANNABEL LEE/THE BELLS

Electronics with bell tones

LENORE
Let the burial rite begin,
The funeral song be sung,
An anthem for the queenliest dead
That ever died so young.

Sweet Lenore has gone before,
Taking hope that flew beside,
Leaving instead the wild dead child
That should have been your bride.

It was many and many a year ago
In a kingdom by the sea,
She was a child and you were a child
In the kingdom by the sea.

But the moon never beams,
The stars never rise,
No angels envy thee,
For Ligeia rests dead
With three winged seraphs
In this kingdom by the sea.

Wedded darkly
Soul to soul
You shrink in size
Down to a mole
And disappear into the hole
Of the dark mind's imaginings.

Shrinking
Shrinking
Shrinking.

HOP-FROG

Hop-Frog (the Dwarf Court Jester)
Well they call me a juicy hop-frog
You can see me in any wood bog
Don't you know that they call me the hop-frog
Hopping frog

I'm a hop-frog
A hop-frog
They call me the hop-frog
Hop . . . Hop-frog

They call me a hop-frog
See me in any wood bog
Don't you know that they call me a hop-frog
Hop-frog

They call me a hop-frog
See me in a wood bog
They're calling me a hop-frog
Hop-frog

You can see me in a ballroom
You can see me in a bedroom

You can see me in the woods
The hop hop-frog

They call me hop-frog
They call you hop-frog
Well they call you hop-frog
Hop-frog
Hop-froggg
Froggggggg

EVERY FROG HAS HIS DAY

Horn melody

KING
O mellifluous dwarf, prince of all the jesters,
Funny little thing you are—
Make me laugh
As God's voluminous star.

HOP-FROG
Gracious majesty, today
Is not made-for-laughter day.
This moment sacred is more for royal sunsets
Than comic ruin or suicidal jests.

KING
I'll be the judge of that, thank you.
Make me laugh le petite cur.
Drink some wine
Lest you foul sweet time.

HOP-FROG
Drink upsets me—please, your liege—
This would mark the death of me.

KING
I said drink, you scabrous whore.
Are you deaf as well as short?

TRIPITENA
Kingdom's sire, big as you are,
Save such bile for larger foes.

KING
Make me laugh
'Fore I stretch your neck like a giraffe.

TRIPITENA'S SPEECH

TRIPITENA

My love. The king by any other name a pissoir. You, my love,
tower over them all; they are but vermin beneath your heels.
They are monkeys. Suit them—frame them to your own vision—but do not let one false word of mockery seep through
to your vast heart. I have seen you from close and afar, and
your worth far exceeds your height, your width, the depth of
your sorrow.

O willful outcast, dost thou not see the light of our love—
our linked fortunes—our hearts melded together into one
fine golden braided finery? They listen to the music of idiots
and amuse themselves with the sordid miseries of their busi-
nesses. They are not the things of angels or of any higher
outpost that humanity might aspire to. Your loathsome
vomitous businessman king is of the lowest order, his advisers
crumbling mockeries of education driven by avarice. My love,
dress them in the suits of mockery, and in their advanced state
of stupidity and senility, burn and destroy them, so their ashes
might join the compost which they so much deserve. If jus-
tice on this earth be fleeting, let us for once hear the weeping
and the braying of the businessman king. Let them be the
orangutans they are and set them blazing from the chandelier
for all to see—hanging from the ceiling by their ridiculous
chains and petticoats, which you will have them wear under

the guise of costumic buffoonery. He who underestimates in time is bound to find the truth sublime and hollow lie upon the grates of systemic disorder.

Businessmen, you're not worth shitting on.

WHO AM I?

TRIPITENA

Sometimes I wonder who am I
The world seeming to pass me by
A younger man now getting old
I have to wonder what the rest of life will hold

I hold a mirror to my face
There are some lines that I could trace
To memories of loving you
The passion that breaks reason in two

I have to think and stop me now
If reminiscences make you frown
One thinks of what one hoped to be
And then faces reality

Sometimes I wonder who am I
Who made the trees
Who made the sky
Who made the storms
Who made heartbreak
I wonder how much life I can take

I know I like to dream a lot
And think of other worlds that are not
I hate that I need air to breathe
I'd like to leave this body and be free

I'd like to float like a mystic child
I'd like to kiss an angel on the brow
I'd like to solve the mysteries of life
By cutting someone's throat or removing their heart

You'd like to see it beat
You'd like to hold your eyes
And though you know I'm dead
You'd like to hold my thighs

If it's wrong to think on this
To hold the dead past in your fist
Why were we given memories
Let's lose our minds and be set free

Sometimes I wonder who am I
The world seeming to pass me by
A younger man now getting old
I have to wonder what the rest of life will hold

I wonder who started this
Was God in love and gave a kiss
To someone who later betrayed
And godless love sent us away

To someone who later betrayed
Godless love sent us away
Someone who later betrayed
Godless love sent us away

COURTLY ORANGUTANS

Electronic court music

HOP-FROG
Tomorrow is the seasonal ball.
I propose costumes for you
And the honorable ministers to wear.

KING
Yes?

HOP-FROG
All dress as orangutans.
All your guests will run and scream
With their mouths agape
And try to hide
And you, sire, will have last laugh
For such imperial cunning.

Ominous low horns
I will redress the wrong.
I will torture you.
I will burn you.
Dead!

TRIPITENA
My prince—
My prince, you light the fire of eternal fame:
BURN MONKEYS BURN!

Loud feedback and electronics—"fire music"

GUARDIAN ANGEL

YOUNG POE AND CAST

I have a guardian angel
I keep him in my head
And when I'm afraid and alone
I call him to my bed

I have a guardian angel
Who keeps bad things from me
The only way to ruin it would be for me not to trust me

The only way to ruin it would be for me not to trust me
I have a guardian angel
Who's often saved my life

Through malevolent storms and crystal drums
The angel on my right
Has lifted me up and set me down
Always showing me what's right

And if my instinct proved me wrong
The angel set it right
And if my instinct proved me wrong
The angel set it right

I have a guardian angel
I keep him in my head
And when I'm having nightmares
He shows me dreams instead

I have a ring—I have a dress
I have an empty shell
By the books below teacups
I've kept a kind of hell
By the books below teacups
I've kept a kind of hell

Panic and anxiety so often in my head
But I had a guardian angel
Who took care of me instead

The champagne cork—the nightlight owl
A raven and a duck
The seed of pining parents
And your despairing love
The seed of pining parents
And your despairing love

Love and luck both having charmed lives
Can change all things about
I had a guardian angel
That's what this is all about

I have a guardian angel
I keep him in my head
When I'm alone and become afraid
He saved my life instead
When I'm alone and become afraid
He saved my life instead